Loup River Psalter

William Kloefkorn

LOUP RIVER PSALTER

by

William Kloefkorn

Spoon River Poetry Press
2001

Loup River Psalter copyright © 2001 by William Kloefkorn. All rights reserved. No portion of this book may be reproduced in any manner without written permission of the author, except for quotations embodied in reviews or articles.

Published by Spoon River Poetry Press, P.O. Box 6, Granite Falls, MN 56241.

Cover photo by Michelle Pichaske.
Editorial assistance, Amy Myers.
Interior drawings by John Kloefkorn.

Printed by Thomson-Shore, Dexter, Michigan.

ISBN: 0-944024-41-6

1 2 3 4 5

CONTENTS

ONE

TWO

THREE

for the Loupers,
then and especially now

ONE

We have a notion that magic resides in a separate and inaccessible world, but magic is with us and contained in reality. It is natural, not supernatural. Power flows from the natural world and the measure of its integrity and of our integrity is the presence of clean running water.

—Richard Manning, *One Round River*

SOON

> *The river. Every time I come here, there it is. Always kind of surprises me, though. Surely it does.*
>
> —Angel Finn in Kent Meyers' *The River Warren*

Soooon is the song
sung by the pickup's tires

on the blacktop, *soooon* you
will be on the river,

gear having *soooon* been
secured

in the jonboat, the canoes,
soooon soooon soooon,

pickup's tires
on the blacktop singing *soooon,*

soooon you will be there,
soooon you will stand

on the bank by the water,
soooon you will be there,

soooon soooon soooon, so
soooon you will cut that

landlubber cord, so *soooon*
you will be on the

river.

LATE EVENING ON THE NORTH BANK

I sit on the bleached-white trunk
of a cottonwood
watching the moon's reflection
in the Loup's slow-moving current.

First a guitar, then a banjo. Red-
haired Boy. Devil's Dream. I
take my turn at the amber bottle,
then pass it on.

Faces in something of a circle
flicker, washed earlier
by water, washed now
by flame.

On the surface of the moving water
a full milk moon, moon
of the shedding ponies,
seems not to move.

I pull an old Barlow from my pocket,
with its silver blade
begin the non-profit business
of essential whittling.

Darkness gathers itself into more
darkness. The whiskey
returns. Peaceful Easy Feeling.
Blackberry Blossom.

The campfire cackles
like an old man
who can't stop remembering
something funny.

LOVE SONG AT MIDNIGHT

If there is magic on this planet, it is contained in water.
—Loren Eiseley, *The Immense Journey*

At midnight
I awaken to the sound

of moving water,
voodoo water, water

with its hocus-pocus never
ending, water that compels

whatever else is chiefly water
to acknowledge change that water

never ending must unendingly
promote,

I awake now in the silent tent
aware of change, this body

chiefly water changing,
voodoo body, body

with its hocus-pocus never
ending, body that arising

moves outside
beneath a yellow moon

to listen more distinctly
to water

moving, water
in me and beneath me

on this shoreline
changing, water

that will take me until it
having done so

further takes me.

STORM

All the rivers run into the sea,
yet the sea is not full.
—Ecclesiastes 1:7

Because we would be prudent
in order to be saved
we pitch our tents
and build a fire

before the storm strikes,
though we do not anticipate
such fury—wind
sufficient to level Omar's tent,

an aftermath of hail that
when the last cloud passes over
proves providential: plenty
of ice now for the drinks, plenty

of drinks now for a trinity
of toasts: here's
to the evening that lies before us
like the dream that follows

evening, to the fire that
somehow in its hard heart's core
retained its heat—and
to the apples of the earth

we'll slice to fry tomorrow
morning, sun rising brilliant
against an eventual rising
of the sea.

POCKET KNIFE

Because I lack the skill
to move beyond the basic pleasure
derived from common whittling

I would purchase talent
by purchasing the knife
I'm wooed to purchase:

Remington, Bulldog, Boker,
Camillus, Case.
Against the palm

I would have handles
of bone, abalone, mother-
of-pearl, shades of oyster,

stag, mastadon ivory, rose,
wildfire, shapes of canoe,
trapper, buckhorn,

muskrat, Jack. O send me
the eternal stainless blade
honed in Solingen, Winchester

with its serrations, pocket
cutlery by Frost, Chicago,
Hen & Rooster, Puma

with its copperlock, scrimshaw,
brass liners, brass pins. O
brothers and sisters

consider not only
the lily of the field
but likewise the dropworts

that are with us always: Buck,
Barlow, and the Uncle Henry
I've settled for

to give this length
of diamond willow another
chance—and myself in turn

another cause to be however
high or low the price
enriched.

ODYSSEY

After my boatmate plugs his ears
he lashes me to the mainmast,
after which he stands an easy distance
in front of me, facing me, ready
to read my lips.

Waiting to hear the first sounds,
however faint, I anticipate
strains too melodious for the human ear,
yet only when they reach me
do I appreciate how
pitifully frail was my expectation.

As best I can I speak aloud
what can't be spoken, my boatmate
studying the movements of my lips
as if their words in silence
might sufficiently inform him—until

those notes too sweet to be resisted
fade into the crosswinds
and the willows
into non-existence.

Later, unlashed and recovered,
I sit near the campfire,
its cottonwood
hissing. Snake, sure enough,
burnt-orange and silver-tongued. Well,
I am only human. I move closer. Then
closer. Then listen.

BREAKFAST

With a flowered towel as apron
and a washcloth as hotpad
our breakfast cook

serves breakfast: flapjacks
whose batter is chiefly beer, bacon
thick-slabbed and crisp, eggs

however you say you like them, black,
black coffee. Biscuits, then,
and tortillas dipped in salsa

for dessert. So who
bent the fucking spatula? Who's
sitting on the fucking salt? The

eggs, seems to me, win the purple
ribbon, so to flatter the cook
I ask for a second round. He

grins like the gopher
I saw last evening between
his tent and mine, breaks

a large white egg into a large
black skillet asizzle with grease.
And Jesus come home

to save us all it's a double-yolker,
each yolk a yellow
deeper than the sun. It's a good omen,

the cook says his almanac says. Shitfire,
he says. Too bad you ain't home
to enjoy some.

EATING LUNCH ON A SANDBAR HALFWAY BETWEEN PALMER AND FULLERTON

Quartering a firm red Jonathan
I cut my left index finger
with the long silver blade
of my Uncle Henry,
blooddrops describing berries
in the hot white sand.

Limbs of cottonwood lie on the tiny island
as if the torsos and the arms
of Picasso's children.
With one strip torn from a blue bandanna
I wrap the finger until the blood
stops oozing,
cold beer then for medication.

Tomorrow, says Johnny the Guru,
might be another day,
and sure enough it is,
lunch on yet another sandbar,
but this time the apple
quarters cleanly,
each tart slice taken to the mouth
with the long silver blade,
apple and the brief cold touch of steel
more admonitive than blooddrops into
berries
against the tongue.

EARLY EVENING

An old man
walks into the campsite
demanding to see our credentials.

Alfalfa greets him, bows deeply,
shakes his hand, with flourishes
shows him our credentials.

The old man, grinning an absence
of teeth, agrees
to stay for supper. Gumbo. French

bread. Peaches. Coffee. Before
the rising of the sun
we will learn that the old man,

by his own account, owns
most of Merrick County,
including the water that flows

this side of an imaginary line
that precisely divides
the river. But for the moment

what we don't know can't
evict us, can it? Credentials
intact, one way or another,

we help ourselves to generous
portions of gumbo, one by one
finding a piece of terrain

not already occupied to sit on.

EPIPHANY

Brother baptizes himself, mostly in
darkness,
by falling from the jonboat
into a font the rest of us call river,
he having been kneeling
aft, near the cooler,
brushing his teeth. Though
well away from the ceremony
we others, speaking in hushed tones
around the campfire,
heard its quaint beginning,
a sudden gargantuan *plop!* we judged to be
the dropping away of another
half acre of shoreline.

Three times, brother tells us, he went
under: in the name of the Father,
the Son, the Holy Ghost.
He is sitting ominously close to the fire,
drying out, his face aglow,
his shin where he cut it against
he doesn't know what
yet bleeding.

When your time comes
to see the light, brother says,
to hell with the darkness: you see it.
In this eurythmic of yin and of yang,
he says, nothing is left to chance.

He is standing now
with his back to the flames,
speaking, it seems, to some point
beyond us in the blackness, his tan
washpants, drying, less and less tan.

We take turns nursing the cut,
with cotton soaking up the ooze.
I didn't retrieve them, he says,
meaning toothbrush and toothpaste.
They are now at one with the river.

Brother smiles. He has gone down
to the water and, having brushed
perhaps too vigorously, has
fallen in. Now he is back
among us, teeth—bridges and all—
in place for tomorrow's epiphany.

BAIT

River fisherman tries whatever's
at hand: chicken guts, liver,
doughballs, blood.

But it's most always the crawler
river fisherman returns to, worm
fat, succulent, worm

fecund with the damp damp earth
it comes from. River fisherman
knows that for every

writhing clot of bait he loses
another is on its way,
nightcrawlers up through soil

just recently rained on
mating, making more bait for
catfish biding their time

eating others eating in the river.

BATHING IN THE CHANNEL

Buck naked and therefore vulnerable,
green jonboat
tethered to a cottonwood
thus far not molested
by beaver,
I bathe myself
until the fresh bar of Ivory

loses the letters of its identity.
If a goddess should happen along,
if I should look up
to see her watching me,
would I be within my mortal rights
to strike her forever
blind?

Sand no longer at home
in the Sandhills
gives way beneath my feet. Sac and horn
float on the water as if bobber
and bait. I extend the lathering
to include the face, the hair.
Eyes closed,

I give myself over to movement,
this body as if the unwieldy log
that because its resistance is low
sooner or later will get there.
When eventually I rise,
when eventually my legs are steadied
against the current,

I will shake the river from my hair
to see already a half moon
skirting the clouds,
and trusting its light
I'll return to the boat
and the cottonwood, to the spot
where the goddess might have stood,

where I will build the fire.

SONG

Bullfrog, bunchgrass, catfish, carp.
Play it with your banjo,
play it on your harp.

If harp means harmonica
the boy will not object
should he be sent
to Heaven. Meanwhile, he
baits a treble hook with liver,
sends the blood-red blob
singing like a sweet soprano
into the water.

Sunset, moonrise, midnight, dawn.
Play it with a grassblade
on your pennywhistle tongue.

Leaving rod and reel to their own devices
the boy, believing
he has music inside him,
positions a grassblade
on his tongue,
spends most of the rest of the day
looking for a possible tune.

And in the tent at night, in the pale moonlight,
you can hear those bullfrogs serenading,
do re mi.

Snagging the bullfrog is not as easy
as some might believe. Dangle
slowly a small feathered lure
in front of the bullfrog's snout.
Shake it. Hope he'll take it
in the blink of an eye
into the cavern of his mouth.

And in the tent at night, in the pale moonlight,
me and my best friend,
Norma Jean.

In back of the tent, behind a cedar,
warm pecker in a cold hand,
the boy would memorize something
to retain the moment: cluster
of stars, nighthawk, shadows
on a three-quarter moon.
Tomorrow, maybe, he'll tell her
one of the many remarkable things
he has learned.

YEAR OF THE FLOOD

During the Year of the Flood I learn
relentless,
having pushed away alone from the shore

unaware of the swift uncanny rising
of the water.
No snag then, no jut of fallen tree,

no sandbar, only a roiling expanse
both to starboard
and port, its movement gauged only

by the dizzy velocity of cutbank and meadow
racing, retreating
upstream, while objects that lie leagues

ahead arise suddenly, unlikely rabbits
pulled upward
from unlikely hats, and I work the oars

only to move Our Lady one nudge at a time
away from where
I guess the channel to be, *relentless*

neck to neck with *inexorable,* all those jokes
about pissant rivers
no longer amusing—until either mirage

or a high stretch of sand not yet overrun
by water
appears in the distance to port, and now

it's dead reckoning by way of devotion, pure
and simple,
may God bless especially the oarlocks

as well as the oars I put everything into,
scratch of sand
against the flat devoted jonboat bottom

happening then too quickly for time to be
measured,
I out of Our Lady and with its bow-line

pulling its sweet dead weight onto the dry
though rapidly
disappearing sand. O how little time it takes

when *relentless* pounds at your cabin door
to move both
gear and boat to the comparative safety

of a grass-bordered shore! Tarp, hatchet,
tacklebox,
tent. I am high and dry. Backpack. Foodbox.

Entrenching tool. Beer. And Body, this body
not moving,
its absence of motion defining *relentless*,

water rising, water not having stopped when
I stopped, water
not stopping when time stops, and we sleep.

GUMBO

The recipe, cook says, is for him
to know and for us
to find out.

So who cares? That is, who
gives a fat rat's ass?
The proof, I say, resides squarely
in the pudding.

Cook stands near the fire
beside a cottonwood
ladling steaming gumbo
into white bowls
with blue barns on their
bottoms. Garlic, yes, and
oysters and tomatoes
and okra. Existence, cook says,
preceding essence. Yes.

Yes, and onion and shrimp
and pepper sauce, I say, and
aroma preceding taste. Yes.

Yes, and crab and rice, I'm
guessing. And parsley and spice
and everything nice. Just guessing.

Cook ladles himself a worthy portion,
soup over rice in a white bowl
with a blue barn on its
bottom. Snakes and snails
and puppy-dog tails. Just guessing.

But who cares? That is, who
gives a fat rat's ass?
Doesn't the proof reside squarely
in the pudding?

DRIFTING

Because we cannot agree on a campsite
we continue to drift
until evening becomes a quarter moon
spilling its necklace of stars
into the river. Carp
we saw earlier in daylight
come to us now
only on the fins
of their obscene sucking.

By now we should be
pitched and secure,
sitting warm by a campfire.
By now we should be
white teeth in a glow
of cottonwood, flash of eye
like a tilt of knife-
blade, cheekbones
radiant.

Downstream to starboard
a small square of light
breaks the darkness. Drifting,
I watch the light
become a window
in a distant farmhouse. Drifting,
I see a figure
moving inside the light,
a woman with long dark hair
wearing only a peach-colored slip.
How can I know this?
How can I know
that she is barefooted,
that she walks
on cool linoleum?
That after we have drifted
not only out of sight
but out of hearing

she will call me in?

FLANNEL

Are these tall leafless stems
here in a marshy overflow
bulrushes? Moses,
sweet baby, where are you?

*

In Sunday-school
our teacher depicted Bible stories
on a flannelboard, perhaps
without intending it
suggesting that what cannot
be represented visually and with flannel
does not exist. Moses exists
because in flannel he lies
in a flannel crib that sits
half hidden among
tall leafless stems of flannel
that bespeak existence. Yellow
the flannel face of Moses, white
the flannel crib, brown the many
flannel leafless stems. Blue, then,
the flannel cutout that
makes a reality of sky.

*

Something about a baby lying in a crib
half sunk in marshwater
squeezed at the heart, squeezing intensified
when the flannel form of Pharaoh
appeared on the board, off to one side
yet walking toward the rushes,
flannel baby and flannel badass
on their way to a deadly
flannel confrontation.

*

I part the tall stems
not to discover the hidden baby
but instead to select a dozen rushes
to form a bouquet
I'll place in a bottle to place on a stump
to dignify the campsite.

*

With flannel our teacher
could breathe the breath of life
into almost anything: camel, shepherd,
prodigal, wise man, Mary, sheep,
oxen, Gabriel, Jonah, samaritan, Daniel
and the lion and the lion's den.
There seemed to be no bottom
to her well of flannel. And when
she took away the scene
behold! the scene
somewhere among the bulrushes
somehow remained.

*

When eventually we circle the fire
to wait for that moment
when the coffee declares itself
finished
I can see through dancing flames
bulrushes dancing. Moses,
sweet baby, where are you? The sky
is a dark flannel sea of bright flannel
stars, beyond them
in flannel not yet cut and placed
the promise of an end to parting.

WIND

This is no circumstance
for old men: oarlock
crippled, a gale-force wind
confronting the face, no matter
which way the face turns.

Yet an early sun
clearly defines the shoreline
and beyond: so thick, so green the leaves,
so white the farmhouse, so red the barn.

Even so, the wind makes a mockery
of the oars,
and O how that one oar
tethered to its lock
augments the mockery, squealing
like an endangered pig
each time I work it
to move the jonboat into whitecaps
I'm guessing overlap the channel.

Yet those primary colors
persist: so pink the far edge
of a lone bank of cumulus,
so blue that vast reminder of the heavens,
so yellow the early rising sun.

Even so, no thanks to this godforsaken
wind, I once again guess wrong: I'm
aground on sand cleverly disguised
as water, water that slap and slaps
steadily as a metronome
against the port side of Our Lady.

Yet there is much to be said
for steadiness, for the sound it makes
in the deepest channels
of the ear. I close my eyes. Slap and slap
says the water against the port side
of Our Lady. Slap and slap and

slowly I can feel the sand beneath me
slowly whorling, slap and
slap and ever so slowly moving. And though
in another week or two, another
month, a year, we'll not be
where at last we mean to be, drifting
whatever river, surely we'll be
always some place near.

FIRE

Mostly hardwood tonight,
limbs of bur oak broken from a tree
undercut by the channel,

until the bed of coals is both
deep and brilliant, above them
flames like the fingers

of a skilled necromancer
reaching to inform the dark.
It is a great fire, truly,

someone says, *truly* spoken like
Hemingway's Santiago might have
said it when talking to his

marlin. It is not a *great* fire,
truly, says someone else. But
truly it is a *good* fire. And

so it goes, great and good
given equal time, until clearly
the circle around the fire sits

divided, the Great Fire People
and the Good Fire People
with their logic and counter-

logic declaiming, reinforcements
called up from time to time
to shore up whatever

shoreline might be sagging—Pro-
metheus, Vulcan, Moses,
Freud, the Sweet Swan of Avon,

Nietzsche, W. C. Fields,
Heraclitus (*One cannot fall into the
same fire twice*)—the flames

meanwhile dying down, almost out,
until both factions as if on
cue arrive at consensus: send

Kent the Rookie out for a fresh
supply of wood. No sound then but
that of water—that

relentless geezer, laughing—and
the intermittent
popgun poppings of bur oak

as Kent the Rookie attends greatly,
or so it seems to me,
to business.

BUSHMILL

Irish whiskey for the Padre
and by the time guitar and banjo
have been fine-tuned

Padre's feet, with Padre above them,
have begun their dancing,
a jig that Padre calls Irish

improvisation—whiskey meanwhile
finding its way
from one flamelit face to another,

finding its way back then
to the one who offered it,
bottle in one hand, cigar

in the other, feet in rapid
and precise improvisation
around the fire and

around again, guitar and banjo
joined now by harmonica
to augment the fever—*O*

you don't shake it like you
used to—Padre quivering
like a Pentecostal dervish,

like a fellow with the heebie-jeebies,
like he has sure enough
ants in his Bushmill pants,

but grinning all the while
like a sophomore, like a gopher,
like if he had a brain

he'd have good sense,
like he'd like to disagree
by way of these contortions

with the words of the tune—*O*
you don't shake it like you
used to

anymore—until the song's sudden
ending seems to startle Padre,
to bring him up short

as if a hidden wire
meant to trip him,
and he falls not into but

over the fire, his body an arch
over the coals,
Bushmill in one hand, cigar

in the other, body a bridge
in stasis absorbing heat,
marking time,

body that when a fresh tune begins
like a Johnny-jump-up
jumps up,

unscathed and free and loose
as Andy the rag doll
out of its cradle,

yet rocking.

SOUTH BRANCH

> *They that go down to the sea in ships, that do business in great waters: these see the work of the Lord, and his wonders in the deep.*
>
> —Psalms 107: 23-24

Not stones down from the mountains
but sandpebbles down from the hills.

Over and under and beside these pebbles
water moves, reducing them to the sand
we reach our oars and paddles down to touch,
to sound the depth of the channel. Mark one
fathom. Mark twain. Or would, but the oar
strikes sand well short of a dozen feet,
though we are pleased and grateful
for what we have, we having come down
to no great sea in no great ships
to do no great business, though works and
wonders from whatever hand do not escape us.

The current tells me with
its sudden maelstroms that I
am moving. Peace is this,
and the quick liquid note
of the meadowlark,
its small sound
hovering like flotsam
on the sun-washed crown
of the river.

We look upstream beyond the reach of seeing
to observe a trinity of sources, North Loup,
Middle Loup, Pomme de Terre. We see a woman
at the edge of a cutbank gathering
tubers. She rises to watch a thin canoe
glide downstream into an infinity of distance.

It is not my no great sea
that I am on, in no great ship
doing no great business
for no one great—except perhaps
for the lark, who perhaps
accepts my sight
as I its sound. How could it
see me except that I be here?

Let us call this south branch Pomme de Terre
is what the Skidi said, their tutors,
the French, beside them, nodding. We must
squint mightily against a lowering sun
to see them. We squint mightily. We
see them.

With one downstretched hand
I give the river bones
to part its current with.
My hair stirs stillness
into a slow cool breeze.
And though just now I
cannot see the lark
can I not hear its
singing? Great waters
are those immediately
beneath us, great ships
those, however scarcely
ribbed, that bear us up.

SONG

Man with the Martin
sings softly to an audience
of warmflesh and firelight:

> *Get back to the well*
> *every now and then,*
> *when your spirit is dry*
> *and your mind is growing dim . . .*

How old was I
when as a boy I
lay on my belly
on cold concrete
drinking water
rising from God
knows where: how
old was I then?

*

It was a spring house
whose spring-fed water
flowed into a creek
that fed into a pond
that provided water
for cattle and horses,
catfish and carp and
unbelievable turtles,
some of them snappers,
all of them at one
time or another
rising to the surface of my
occasional dream:
how old was I then?

*

Man with the Martin
sings softly to an audience
of owlcall and starshine:

You don't have to run
with the Joneses,
whoever the Joneses
might be . . .

Who knows or cares
who owned and managed
the spring house,
whose cattle and horses
drank at the spring-fed
pond? Their names
no less than their land
have been sold
to the highest bidder,
and so on.

*

That long afternoon
when with nightcrawlers
I caught the world's
largest catfish
I couldn't stop
talking, *Jesus Christ*
my only mark
of punctuation. When
later, ready
to call it a day,
I hauled in the stringer
to see only bones
and distended eyes
on a huge head mostly mouth,
I couldn't say anything
more than *turtle*. There
wasn't anything
more to say.

*

Man with the Martin
sings softly to an audience
of tincup and ashglow:

And you begin to think
it's time your time has come.
Get back to the well
from where your spirit has come.

On the way home
I stopped again
at the spring house
to drink the cold
running water. As
I drank I looked far
down to see the shining
pebbles the water
seemed to be rising
from, looked harder
then to see what might
lie beyond. Source, I
thought. And I thought,
Where does the source
of the first source
come from?

*

Many times as a boy I kicked
the same rock
all the way
from the spring house
to the back door
of my backwoods home.
And there was magic
in the rock and
in the kicking and
in the clean running
water as I lay on cold
cement in the spring
house drinking, magic
too in warmflesh and
firelight, owlcall and
starshine, tincup and
ashglow: as a boy

how old am I now? Christ
Jesus! How old
was I then?

TWO

I find myself, out there in the middle of the wide river, the wild world, relishing and rolling around my palate and striving to grasp and fix in memory the cadence of the river's rhythm with its themes and variations that are echoes of wider themes and variations.

—Colin Fletcher, *River*

YEAR OF THE DROUGHT

We count off, odds going
to their knees to pray, evens
going out in search of wet sand.

These efforts thus far not
successful
we circle our waists with bow-lines

to begin the modern miracle
of navigating white
hot sand.

So this is what the Sandhills
look like when their
prodigals leave home,

nineteen thousand square miles
of fertile dunes
one grain at a time coming down.

We tug until our modern miracle
wanes,
encouraging us to shed

everything but our collective skin—
until drag has the final
word. We know, we know:

in the beginning it was water
we put into, but water
that somehow wandered off

when our backs were turned. On
my way to collapsing
I notice: on this sandbar

we are not alone: driftwood
of every shape imaginable, here
and there a complementary bone.

INSTRUMENTAL

At the moment it's *All in G*
on the banjo, notes
precise, cat-quick and clean
sent out and up
to whatever has ears to listen.

Without words the message
makes consummate sense,
without words no tower
with its forked, dissenting
tongues babbling.

Maybe this is pretty much
the way it was meant to be,
if anything is,
melody the sole arbiter
leveling pride and prejudice,

spite and greed, deceit and
inhibition. O brothers and sisters!
In the beginning was the word
restrained, its deadly decipherings
on hold until the music stops

and the word like the snake it
so often is
returns.

THE SMALL ANIMAL

The small animal
I almost stepped on
has a heart
beating now more rapidly
than I thought possible,
in my hand its soft
grey body all
heartbeat and tremble.

I know, I know:
all along
this shoreline thicket,
in partial sunshine
or absolute shadow,
hearts beat at the expense
of others' hearts. So
what does it matter
where the intruder
steps?

Say it matters. Say
you are near a river,
in a thicket
chiefly of locust and pine,
on your way to discovering
a spent branch suitable
for whittling. Say
you discover instead
this creature you have
no name for. Say

you lift it in your palm
to name it, its
fear and its heartbeat
overwhelming you
with their absence
of power. Say,
having named it—Heartbeat,
Tremble—you

release it into the vagaries
of overgrowth and underbrush.
Say you have not forgotten
what you are about, that
somewhere a spent branch
waits to be lifted. Say that,
uplifted or otherwise,
it matters.

CIRCUMSTANTIAL

Some circumstantial evidence is very strong,
as when you find a trout in the milk.
—Thoreau, *Walden*

Yes, or leviathan
in the Loup, though I didn't find it
myself, someone else did, or

said he did—not find it
but see it, he said, and
not near at hand

but at a distance, though distance
can be tricky on the river,
especially in the heat of the day

when everything at a distance
shimmers—but he did see
it, he believes, creature

rising from the water
too mammoth to be believed
if by belief one means logic

or synthesis or paradigm. Look,
he says, he saw it, maybe
a beast, maybe serpent, maybe fish,

in any case something the size
of West Texas, and Jesus Christ on
a popsicle stick

isn't that enough? he asks
while drinking what he claims to be
his first boilermaker of the evening.

WHERE IS BOY?

I don't recognize Lord Greystoke
until he removes his tie and coat,
trousers and shirt and shoes
and those disgusting almost
knee-high black rayon socks,
leaving him covered only
with a loincloth and, of course,
sufficient hair to suggest
the primate.

He is looking for Cheetah who,
he says—reverting chiefly
to gutterals—eloped,
he suspects, with Jane.

As it turns out I alone
am in a position to help him,
saying that, yes, I believe
I saw her late last night. She
was with someone who looked to be
something perhaps not quite us,
both of them floating the river
in a silver canoe. They
looked my way, but I'm certain
they didn't see me,
though a half moon was shining,
and though it all happened
so very slowly.

He grimaces, beats his chest
with both fists, lets loose a yell
both remote and familiar. I alone,
I believe, understand his pain.

His eyes dart quizzically
this way and that from one treetop
to another. No, I say, the
limbs on the trees here—cottonwood,
willow, bur oak, pine—have
no vines for swinging.

He nods, smiles thinly, offers his
hand. I shake it. Tarzan thank you,
he says, and before I can ask Where
is Boy? he has run to the nearby
shore where for only a moment
he pauses before diving
into the current. I watch him
disappear quickly downstream and
around a bend, his other identity—lying
meanwhile in a heap beside me—unlikely
as the next time it happens
can hope to be.

CAR BODIES

Birds above,
a funeral below. Poetry.
—Paul Eggers, *Saviors*

Along an extended stretch of lazy river
upturned car bodies from a last line
of resistance, metal bastion
intended to deflect the current to eat
away the shoreline of someone else's pasture.

On the hood of an old green Catalina
Chief Pontiac thrusts
his sleek silver head
with its sleek silver hair
upward into the eye of a clear morning's sun.

I squint to see if anything here
resembles the Bel-Air Chevy
I and my sweetie made love in,
one of our bare lustful feet
breaking the glass on the domelight.

In less than a moment it is evening,
rookie off on his own
after firewood,
veterans with martinis
talking supper. If we had a clear-channel

radio, and if the day were Valentine's, 1945,
we could tune in and listen—to the baritone
of Crosby singing *Don't Fence Me In*, maybe,
or reports of the firebombing, muted
but intense, of Dresden.

WRONG

Padre says that
nothing is more wrong than the wound
that denies forever the wild bird's flight.

Nothing more wrong than the startled, land-
locked body that walks the shoreline
dragging its dumb useless wing

along a gathering deck of composting leaves.
Not pitiful, altogether, or ultimately
sad—just wrong, wrong, wrong,

its wrongness augmented by dark
inevitability: something out there hungry
looking for something wrong.

Which is why the Padre
tracks down the bird to kill it, a mercy
intended to take the lopsided

and straighten it out until, except in the dark,
it sits level—an ornament of note—on the
cosmetized lawn of the scheme of things.

A TRUNCATED HISTORY OF THE CIVILIZING OF MAN

In the old days, when mammoths
stalked the earth and the sloth
hung plentiful, Spanky,
on his way to becoming Man,
with a single boatoar
spanked a giant carp, that same stroke
beheading and scaling and filleting
the giant fish, so that Spanky
had only to roll the flesh
in an off-white mixture
equivalent to flour, to cook it then
on rocks kept steaming
over an open fire.

On his haunches, Spanky, becoming Man,
ate his first carp slowly, delicately,
repast having been this once
devoid of fanfare. On his haunches
he sat facing the water
from which the giant fish had been
delivered. With fingers akin to thumbs
he ate until the last tender morsel
had been consumed, then
tasting his lips with his tongue
Spanky walked sated and upright
into the current of the river,
there to swim far into the day

with a dark exhilaration he had
somehow never felt the
full force of
before.

CAPSIZED

> *Going into Cairo, we came near killing a steamboat which paid no attention to our whistle and then tried to cross our bow. By doing some strong backing, we saved him; which was a great loss, for he would have made good literature.*
>
> —Mark Twain, *Life on the Mississippi*

According to the survivors
it was a water serpent
disguised as a cottonwood branch
that capsized the canoe, serpent
breathing fire, serpent
with malice on its mind,

survivors standing now
on the bank, describing the serpent,
saying what raced through
their own minds
when the canoe went over,
one survivor thinking revenge,

other survivor thinking guitar,
thinking I'm not Jesus
help me
coming up without it, breath
held, eyes open, hands
groping, would rather God forgive me

drown than lose the Martin
to the river,
other survivor meanwhile
thinking revenge, believing too
in the urgency of his quest, his
staying under until he spies a serpent

disguised as a cottonwood branch,
at which spying
he'll twist its deceptive neck
until it hisses *Uncle!*, other survivor
standing now on the bank
pouring river from the hollow

of his guitar, river and an occasional
catfish, survivor grinning,
triumphant,
saying that when the Martin dries
it'll play sweeter than ever,
other survivor standing

not far away, nodding,
blue eyes limpid, warm blood
flowing in undeniable streamlets
from the fang and tooth-
marks on his remaining
arm.

ROPE

Give a river rat enough rope
and having hanged himself
he'll ask for more—always
something to bundle up, tote,
tie down, suspend, subdue.

Here is the vow I have kept,
intend to go on keeping: never
to leave a hardware store
without having bought at least one
of the following—hammer, pliers,
screwdriver, rope.

Let them accumulate, moil, cross-
breed, multiply,
Paradise being that place where
what is most fundamental
lies easily and eternally
within reach.

I meanwhile back-paddle
the starboard oar,
pull stoutly a couple of times
on the port, now with both oars
move Our Lady out of the current
into the slower water along the shore.

There's a lone stump whose denomination
I can't pinpoint just over there.
Using the bow-line as lariat
I'll fetch that stump,
secure Our Lady further with a rope I'll
half-hitch to the stern. If
there's such a rope handy. If—there
goes the stump already!—I can Holy
Mother of the Padre's Jesus
find one.

ALFALFA

. . . the old human story: as individuals, so much greatness and glory, so much to love: in bulk, so gross, so much to deplore.
—Colin Fletcher, *River*

In under seven minutes
he explicates from memory
an unabridged edition of *Ulysses*,
then as an afterword
farts, in the key of C, *Amazing Grace*.

*

Amazing. Grace. Who isn't here,
except at night in the form of moon, moon
whose form, I'm told, is always
female.

*

Alfalfa, squatting,
worries the breakfast coals
with a firebrand. Overhead,
a misbegotten goose
honks its loneliness.

*

She wanted to be here, wanted
to work those selfsame oars
worked by her lover
before his heart so suddenly,
so violently
burst.

*

He knows a story, Alfalfa does,
about the first men
ever to hear the honk of a goose.
Half of them, says Alfalfa,
believed the sound
came from the beak, the others that
it derived from the movement
of the wings. Discussion turned
to heated debate, debate

to dare, dare to open hostilities,
until, bloodied and irrevocably
divided, one group took to the water,
the other vowing to remain on land.

*

We tell her what surely
already she knows: she's a woman.
And because she's a woman
she's a moonchild and
cannot understand.

*

Then once upon a sunrise, says
Alfalfa (with a gloved hand
removing the skillet
from the heat, with a spatula
lifting bacon
enough for a small battalion
onto a brace of piepans), the
Water People and the Land People
chanced to meet. Each contingent
fought to the last man,
then these two fought to their
respective extinctions. Amen.

*

It's my turn
to do the eggs. The skillet
sits ready on the grill,
grease almost sizzling. When
I lift the first egg I wonder:
should I break it in the center,
or at the small, or perhaps
the larger, end?

SHOE

I am the shoe I threw away last summer, man,
on the river, man, man floating
in a jonboat in a current of the Loup, man,
man who in a burst of anger
or maybe deep delight
tossed the shoe into the channel, man,
man who thought he'd never see the shoe
again, man, man with one shoe on,
one shoe off, man, O I am the shoe
I threw away last summer, man,
man drifting now wherever
those tides of fortune and misfortune
take me, man, I am that
unable-to-toss-myself-away man, man,
O I am the shoe I threw away last summer, man,
I am the fit, man, the perfect fit, the
go-to-meeting man, man, man wearing himself
in spite of himself, man, heel to toe, man,
toe to heel, man, forward march column left
to the rear, man, man going hey and diddle-diddle
straight up the middle, man, man
in the middle, man, O man, O shoe, O river,
don't let the bastards ever (do you hear me?)
wear you down.

BOATMATE

My boat is a green jonboat
christened Our Lady of the Loup
with a bottle of Lone Star beer.

Loaded to the gills
it nonetheless draws no more
than five or six inches of the current
we drift in.

I sit at the oars
facing aft. So tell me, boatmate,
where we're headed. Then ask me, boatmate,
where we've been.

We take turns at the oars,
the one on relief reading the channel.
And when just now we find one, wide and deep,
I rest the oars, lean back,
ask my boatmate to fetch me a beer.

In four brief months his heart
will burst too suddenly, too
violently for anything
short of divine intervention
to save him. But today, this hour, this

moment he sits like an unlikely ornament
near the stern of Our Lady.
At his left the shoreline
replete with cattle and crops,
houses and trees and barns and beyond them
a blue-topped horizon
moves swiftly upstream,

and drunk am I before having finished
this first libation—not Lone Star, now,
but something else, something
filled with the ripeness of sun
and of motion, motion
uncanny with change into change,
yet empty of premonition.

REQUIEM

The leaves on the fallen cottonwood
are lime,
in my mouth a tartness
like the juice from the
quickened pace of time.

I stand beside the river
on a patch of solid earth
beside a sapling
stout as a farm boy's arm,
above me a gathering of branches
deciphering the wind:

from the moment
of our first rising up
we are
falling down.

COYOTE

That which doesn't kill you makes you stronger.
—Nietzsche

We first dead-man, then ditch, the tent,
because lightning upriver
has been moving closer,
plus something in the air beyond the lightning—

a sudden cooling, a lapse of breeze, a delicate
moistening. And it's not
the voice of the turtle I hear
but the howl of a coyote, returning me

to my grandfather's farm where standing
on a rock atop the hill
the farmhouse leaned into
I watched dark late-afternoon clouds

roil toward me, coyote having announced them,
clouds with a mind
not possible to read,
and what catches the eye even more

than the curious cobalt lining the clouds
is the blue pickup
parked below
in the valley, a man standing behind it

looking out and over a golden wheatfield,
his hat in his hand ready
at the last moment,
should that moment arrive, to admit it.

SWAMPING OUR LADY OF THE LOUP

Such a talent, my brother says,
such a talent it takes
to swamp the jonboat on a river
smooth as a channel cat's belly,
on a day so clear you can see a baby sawyer
ten leagues away. We are under a cottonwood drying,
gear enough strung out to start a store. My brother,
who smokes but no longer drinks,
speaks eloquently about how difficult it must have been
not to have missed that bone-white thrust of log.
I remind him that we failed to miss it
together.

To steady the nerves I pour myself a drink,
my dream of catching a trophy fish for supper
forever slipping into the current with my tacklebox,
the rod and the reel not more than a poor boy's fathom
behind. The truth is, I don't care. My brother and I,
we hit the bone-white jut of log
smack at the portside center of the boat,
hit that sweet Caucasian erection
together.

Always to be on the lookout
is always to be at the edge of being
undone. Under a high Nebraska sky
how the tentpoles glisten! So who do we think
we are, anyway, God's only gift to creation?
It's our mother's voice
taking us down a notch or two,
its tone split like a crow's tongue,
one half sharp with condemnation,
the other thankful to the point of tears
that we escaped with our own skin. So
here we are, my brother and I, drying out,
everything we own this side of sophistication
coming around. And tonight—
tonight I'll lie awake until early morning
inhaling the stars, within my reach my brother
sober as a judge,
the wind in the leaves of a cottonwood
aromatic as moist tobacco and as
steady as the hymn of grace
I can't for the very life
of either of us remember.

MOCKINGBIRD

Now the mockingbird,
in an effort to be too much of itself,
mocks more than it can handle,

egret and gull,
heron and warbler and shrike,
its throat encumbered with sound,

until arriving at the char char char
of its own dark mind
it mocks itself,

swelling the gullet,
exploding the lungs,
scattering bone and feather

all the way to the south-bank
current in the river,
where the water, pipeline

to something more than itself,
carries them (each fleck
of white and of grey

at the end of a slanting sun
so conspicuous, in this other flight
so definitively absorbed)

out and down to where the bridge
rides high on the crest of its
shadow before going under.

SANDBAR

Sandbar down from the Sandhills
reaches to detain the jonboat.
We sit then, my boatmate and I,
high on a hillock of pebbles

fine almost as sugar, tongues
meanwhile sweetened
with an absolute absence
of motion—except

for those gatherings of cumulus
above, moving, I'd guess, due
north-northeast, and
intending, I'd guess, eventually

to thicken and to darken
until, having given us adequate
warning, they'll release (I'm
guessing) rain enough to impress

both the tent and its maker—our
colleague, Omar, awake
with his fingers like claws
on the tentpoles,

his hands to his arms
to his torso
reinforcements
amounting to mercy.

TRINITY

Because today the sun reveals the stone
that might otherwise have lain
another slow millennium
unrevealed
I worship the sun. What better reason
to reverse a trend?

Because the stone with its heft
impresses the hand, with its
freckles of mica
amazes the eye
I worship the stone. What better reason
to address the end?

Because the water flows on when I give it the stone
that might otherwise never
have been so
scoured
I worship the flow. The reason? For flesh
to guess at. For spirit to know.

CATFISHING

Catfishing on the Loup
I land a Gideon Bible
dry and secure
inside the miracle
of a plastic Ziploc bag.

Is my dark-eyed brother the sweet
peckerhead responsible? He says, No.
He says that his innocence, behold,
runs whiter than the driven snow.

One of my sons asks the following:
What did you use for bait? Blood?
Chicken guts? Liver? I tell him:
nightcrawler.

That evening, near a campfire,
we indulge Virgilian lots,
opening the Bible at random
and, with eyes diverted,
pinpointing a verse: *And*
Jesus said, leave her alone.
Why troublest thou her? She
hath wrought on me a good thing.

Around midnight the other son
returns to the fire
holding high a four-pound
channel, its long body
luminous in a glow of cottonwood coals.

It was Mary of Bethany, someone says,
who sacrificed a portion
of costly ointment,
with it anointing the head of Jesus.
And why not? Soon he
would be sacrificed and, unlike the poor,
there would not be another
to replace him. He said so himself.

I open another beer. I ask my son,
What variety of bait
enticed the channel? Liver?
Chicken gut? Nightcrawler? He tells me:
Gideon.

Someone stirs the coals to life
with a short length
of honeylocust. It came
from the same indifferent tree
I'll happen upon
in the morning, brisk hike
in dubious combat with a hangover.
It'll be that branch just over there:
I'll see it as the walking-stick
one day I'll lean on,
thorns on its white wood
sanded smoothly to freckles,
and I'll touch them with the reverence
that comes each night
when the last of the fire is gone.

WILLIAM TELL OVERTURE

Los Angeles (AP)—Clayton Moore, the masked man who played the Lone Ranger on radio and television, died of a heart attack Tuesday. He was 85. . . . Tonto was played by Jay Silverheels, who died in 1979.

—News item

On his milk-white horse the Lone Ranger,
followed closely by Tonto,
rides into the campsite,
rescues the heroine
and punishes the villain and,
having left a glistening bullet
for all of us to find and wonder over,
gallops into the sunset,
hi-yo Silver and *getemup Scout*
clip-clopping into the ear
like distant and recurring echoes.

*

This early morning, looking
for a sun-cured branch
to whittle on,
I might in fact be walking over
the bones of the Pawnee and the Sioux,
Pawnee who, with their bundles of sacred corn,
became, wherever they were, the center
of the universe, and the Sioux who,
with their arrows and knives of stone,
and later their sacred rifles,
massacred their brothers
to rob and deplete them—

and the Skidi, that blood relative
of the Pawnee,
who given a choice
would have named this moving water
Its Kari Kitsu, Plenty Potatoes River,
edible tubers having grown along the banks
in wild abandon.

*

When finally a promising branch reveals itself
I cut it down to take it with me
back to the campsite
where with my Barlow
I'll work a transformation—something only
to look at, maybe, or something that
when the thundering hoof-
beats of the present
become the past

I'll lean on.

WOODSHED

Tonight my brother, high
on sobriety,
improvises another verse
to add to those other verses
improvised by others:

> *Now Larry had a sister,*
> *The sister's name was Nan.*
> *When Larry smacked his sister,*
> *He took his whuppin' like a man.*

Tonight my brother sings
like the wolf must have sung
on its way to naming the river,
my brother's voice
like the voice of the wolf
unrepentant because untamed.

> *Take your whuppin' like a man, boy.*
> *Take your whuppin' like a man.*
> *Get your ass on down to the woodshed*
> *And take your whuppin' like a man.*

O how easy it would be tonight
to fall in love with sound,
with the human voice
sending its sweet vibrations
upward to whatever heaven—treetop,
nighthawk, cirrus, moon. All of us
going to or coming back from
the woodshed, all of us
doing so divinely again what
all creatures here before
have divinely done.

SONG

I am haunted by waters.
—Norman Maclean, *A River Runs Through It*

When I need to walk,
I'll walk with the river.
When I need to talk,
I'll talk with the river.

The boy doesn't yet know it
but he will be haunted
for the rest of his life
by what he's in love with:
not largeness in the form
of Missouri or Mississippi,
but smallness in the form
of Niobrara, Elkhorn, Loup.

Today he wades the water
of Sand Creek, his bare feet
touching not stones or even
pebbles, but sand so fine
he'll not feel its likeness again
for half a lifetime.

The yellow sand plum
is better off jelly.
The prickly pear
is best left alone.

Embarrassing, isn't it,
to be carrying a black lunch bucket
while others your age
are eating hot lunches, some
at school, others downtown. Even so,
the taste of sand-plum jelly,
at the time and later, as the taste
persists, makes embarrassment
worthwhile. And the bread,
so hot from the oven—the boy
can smell it late into
each afternoon.

The buffalograss
will make a fine cover.
The wild prairie rose
ain't seen, it's discovered.

When Sand Creek runs dry
the boy walks the lowest gully
where water should be. In bare feet
he discovers warmth
from the earth up. Looking at the sky,
blue and endless, he wonders
how much it will rain
when the next rain
comes around.

The cottonwood seed
so lightly dropping
delays its descent,
pausing and stopping.

Some of the cottonwood branches
are brittle, some as dense, it seems,
and as unyielding, as rods
of steel. The boy,
about to strike a match to start a fire,
wonders why. And those bass
jumping now in the pond: when the boy
casts a jitterbug among them
why don't they bite?

When I need a friend
I can count on the river.
Drifting along,
Mother Nature delivers.

The spring house: each time
the boy goes there
there it is. So too the pond.
Each time, surprised, he
stands on the bank
for a long time,
taking everything in. And
though there is too much
ever to be taken in
he takes it in.

THREE

One night, sitting on that river, on the bank, just me and Gruber, saying things once in a while, and generally saying nothing, I thought: This is the way it's supposed to be—just sitting here, talking if you want to, the water going by, and sand eroding off the banks, and trees weakening and falling.

—Luke Crandall in Kent Meyers' *The River Warren*

DIALOGUE

He tells me more than he intended,
or so he tells me.
I am very careful not to tell him
I'm doing the same.

It's the river's fault, river
with its own subdued babbling—and
each moon's fault, too,
that one adrift above, that

other one adrift below, both
tugging shoreward our tides
of speech. Yes, but Jesus isn't this
damn near the perfect evening? So

go ahead, tell me something else
beyond the limit maybe
you set yourself for telling.
What's funny is that later

I'll not remember any of those
dark pearls of revelation—only
that for a brief time they
existed, while we sat

on low stumps that Jesus
once upon a time were maybe part
of some other man or rodent's
damn near perfect evening.

ROUND RIVER

I'm as ready to believe
in the roundness of this river
as in any other roundness,
Sioux holy man having claimed that
all things aspire to roundness, others
insisting that what we give to the river,
both bad and good, returns in other forms
to haunt and uplift us—and that's
roundness, too, I suppose, roundness
as minus, roundness as plus, roundness
occurring regardless of whether
credits keep pace with debits.

> *Yin and Yang fell into the river,*
> *the river ran into the deep blue sea.*
> *The sea joined its essence to the ocean,*
> *now Yin and Yang are falling down on me.*

During the Year of the Ark
we zipped ourselves into tents and bags,
determined to outlast the rain, only one
of our crew willing to rig a tarp
and attempt a fire, thereafter
drying the gear of whoever
could foot the bill—one jigger of joyjuice
for each dry item. From tent to tent
he made the rounds, tents
in a crooked circle, inhabitants
awake and asleep dreaming roundness.

Now the rainwaters have gone their many
and separate ways, yet rumors of rain
persist, our faith in cycles intact
because of the history of cycles.
On a clear day I can see the current
far downriver crossing
to the opposite shore, can follow it
until it reaches the edge
of the known and visible world,
then disappears.

CONNECTIONS

Sometimes, no matter what
you say or do to the contrary,

every damn thing goes right,
the center holds, the pieces

come together, that pastel pink
at the edges of the clouds

at sunset so precisely the color
of the inside of the shell

Grandmother placed on the linoleum
to keep the front door open,

shell she told me to hold to my
ear if I want to learn the sound

the sea makes, its sound so
nearly that of this evening's

moving water, Loup and sea, cloud
and shell, Grandmother in a big boat

rocking on the high seas from Karlshuld
to Kansas to the living-room

where rocking she put together the
cloud-white spread with its patterns

of stars so intricate I sleep
when the other stars don't show

so warmly under.

THE WITCHING HOUR

> *To me an ancient cottonwood is the greatest of trees*
> *because in his youth he shaded the buffalo and wore a*
> *halo of pigeons, and I like a young cottonwood*
> *because he may some day become ancient.*
> —Aldo Leopold, *A Sand County Almanac*

Yonder, legs hanging over the edge
of the riverbank, attaboy sculptor
sits with a length of cedar
carving another miniature
rendition of the human form.

It's the witching hour, everyone
sated, everyone doing what
each one pleases.

I find a spot in the shade,
settle my back against a smooth
curvature of debarked cottonwood,
open my abridged copy of *The*
History of Damn Near Everything.

I'd like to learn more
about the evolution of the zerk,
but it's the witching hour
and I'm not above being bewitched.
I think of Thucydides, or was
it Aristotle, who wrote that
happiness is what finds you when
you're loafing up to your potential.

I therefore in pursuit of happiness
close first the book, next the eyes,
at which moment
I learn again what Longinus, or was it
Paul the Apostle, knew all along,
that clean water, moving, provides,
for the common idler,
the natural world's most delicious sound.

I'm like this tree that is
rooted by the water: until
something more than what's happening
happens,
I shall not be moved.

THE OTHERS

Say that for a few moments
the brain reverts to become the lizard's,
and belly slick against the wet late-night grass
I hear the wind in the cottonwoods
singing an old hymn—

No matter. Lying belly-down on bunchgrass
wet and becoming wetter,
studying the orange in a deep bed of coals,
I hear the hymn, and Christ
I want to wake the others to hear it, too,

but I know that for a long time,
since before the clouds came in
to cover Venus,
the others have been asleep—tentflaps
secure, their breathing

beautifully heavy,
so I listen alone until the song is done,
then rising I walk to the river's edge
to hear the clapping of water
against the boats—

and because a thinning of clouds
expands the night
I move into the river to find the channel
to drift with my belly up with all the others

to catch the moon.

YEAR OF THE PURLOINED CATFISH

No turtle this time, catfish
numerous and large-bellied
having been secured in a sack
with a weave too dense
for Houdini, sack
then tethered to a root
and left suspended in the near-
shore water of the Loup.

Yet fact is tough to observe
directly, then
deny. The catfish have disappeared,
evaporated, vaporized, combusted,
or, what is most likely,
have been lifted
by a desperate intruder: hunger,
Poor Richard might have said, never
knew unreachable bread.

And it is not the absence of fish
for supper that rankles—it's
the question, the puzzle,
the riddle
defying the highest reach
of collective ratiocination.

Until the somewhat apparent
becomes the conclusively obvious:
our catfish, purloined
or otherwise, are not likely
to reappear.

And so it is that mystery
evolves to myth,
our delectable catfish becoming the axle
our speculations spin on,
most of them at last sacred
if not out-and-out divine.

AFTER

After the banquet,
after the awards and toasts and tributes,
after the tears induced by smoke, after the flapdoodle,
after the Padre's everlasting benediction,

someone drags a massive system of cedarroots
onto the coals beneath the smoke,
and as the fire rebuilds itself
we settle into the laconic business
of a long night's journey into morning.

And because our lead guitarist
has the gumbo blues
we have them too,

and because the one with the magic banjo
has those slow-current, deep-water,
look-out-I'm-goin'-under blues
we have them too,

and because the harmonica says *Do me a river, Lord,*
winding and long—just do me a river,
I'll do you a song
we do a song too,

cedarroots warming to the occasion, snapping
their flaming fingers, river
having been done
still doing, still keeping one note at a time
its promoter's half of the bargain.

BIRD

Nobody here knows the name
of that long-necked bird
perched on a length of driftwood
lying high and dry on a sandbar
in the middle of the river.
Who has the bird book?
Who hid the binoculars?

And nobody here perhaps has arm enough
to reach it with these small
green apples that, though
we have them in abundance,
nobody here has desire enough
to throw. Look,

nobody here wants to hit the bird,
nobody wants to hurt it,
only to startle it into flight
so that we might watch and admire
its wide wings as they lift
its impossible weight

to carry it low over water
whose creatures thrive too plentiful
to count, too removed
from what we drifters
deem as pertinent
to know their names.

SHAKESPEARE

Not the Bard of Avon
but an old open-faced reel
handed down from an old open-
faced man who knew a hawk
from a handsaw, who
sitting in his easy chair
was always less asleep
than dreaming—

not of this river but
of that spring-fed pond
in his final days
he haunted the shore of,
bass in the morning
and early evening,
catfish at night
into dawn—

so at the stroke of midnight
I check my line: it is
braided low-stretch dacron,
and something has taken it
halfway into the nearest town.
With the Shakespeare
I reel it in, thread the hook
with an obese worm. Heaven—

it's what lies above
those vast uncountable things
our pitiful philosophies
never dwelt on. And
likewise it's what lies below,
as the Bard of Walden said,
it being under the soles of our feet
as well as over our heads.

NIGHTCRAWLERS

I know only as much
as I need to know
to catch them,

first, that the early summer
months are best, those days
before a prolonged sun
crusts the backyard,

next, that rain is necessary,
rain preferably at night,
slow cool steady rain
soaking gently the short grass
in the backyard,

third, that a flashlight
muted with tissue
enables you to see them
without warning them away,
though you must
walk slowly, and crouched,
and you must be cat-quick
when you make your move or
cat-quick back
to where they came from
they'll disappear.

On a good late night
expect with patience to harvest
six or seven dozen. In
the damp and the darkness
they rise from separate nearby
holes to screw, one
long slick body tightly
joined against the other,
tipping thus the scales of survival
slightly in favor of the hunter.

Almost midnight. In the backyard
I move slowly, playing a muted beam
on clipped fescue before me.
At my right and left
my small sons crouch, moving with me
slowly. They are sharp-eyed,
cat-quick. Cat-quick
they will interrupt six or seven dozen
crawlers mating. They will drop them
into a large coffee can
half filled with porous mulch that
in the hand without the light
I'm holding.

NOT LONG BEFORE SUNSET

I'll not arise and go now
to the Lake Isle of Somewhere Else
because I'm perfectly happy just where I am,
sitting here free of wattles and clay
on a prediluvian stump in the shade
of many cedars, no call for camouflage,
bovines as if curious cousins
grazing the bunchgrass.

It's mid-May, windless and warm,
not long before sunset,
and I'm here for the moment alone,
unable to detect a cricket from a linnet,
an ignorance that extrapolated from sufficiently
might lead to a heightened definition of delight.

O how this waning afternoon does smell
like prairie earth, like honeycomb,
like leaves just moments earlier
rained on. Like white wine,
another portion of which I'll quietly deplete
before nightfall, before Orion strings his bow,
before this body in a certain
slant of moonlight
begins to glow, then glows.

THE DEER

The deer comes to the edge
of the river to drink.
Its ears straighten suddenly
to tell it how harmless
I have become.
Its breath against the water
further softens the early evening.
I have moved away from the bank
to shadow myself
against the bark of a cottonwood
for the rest of my life
to watch this.

BLUES

Music is silence.
The reason we have the notes
is to emphasize the silence.
—Dizzy Gillespie

Our lead guitarist, preacher's boy
out from the wilds of Oklahoma,
fits a capo to the neck of his Martin,

then after some acoustic calisthenics
moves into a litany
of blues—Hesitation Blues, Sweet Baby

Blues, Gambler's Blues—lead guitarist
by himself
on a campstool downstream

singing the blues to anything not
outright opposed to listening. Asks
the bullfrog, How long do I have to

wait? Can I get you now, or mama
do I have to hesitate? Tells the
bunchgrass, She can search

the whole world over, she'll never
find a man like me. To the
catfish: Five long years

with just one woman,
and she had the nerve to kick me
out. To the carp: I love my baby,

love to watch her walk
across the room. Lead guitarist
let loose from Oklahoma

picks and sings as if in concert
at the Met, his audience
of bullfrog, bunchgrass, catfish, carp

quiet as stones with appreciation. And
O how the notes accentuate
the silence! I close my eyes

to hear it more clearly,
make of my hands two vessels devoid
of wrath and spite to take it in.

I tell you, brother, sister, something here
sure as sin is happening, something here
Lordy Lordy is going on!

MIDNIGHT, WHILE MY COLLEAGUES SLEEP

I hear them long before I see them,
laughter and occasional words
so distinct I'm tempted

to join them, which of course I don't,
their being Lord only knows
how many leagues

upstream. So under a remarkable
clustering of stars I sit
on dewgrass and wait,

moon of the shedding ponies waning,
yet bright enough for
silhouettes,

profiles as distinct almost as their
laughter, their words,
and when I wave

they don't wave back, they don't see
me, they are oblivious
to everything

but themselves, as they should be,
young man, young woman
in a silver canoe

drifting the Loup, afraid of nothing,
snag of whatever denomination
be damned, their joy

giving me joy I can't explain, so I'll
not even try, not even
in the morning

at the advent of breakfast, stars and
moon, man and woman
and silver canoe

gone with the laughter and the words
so distinct I'm tempted,
come nightfall,

to join them.

MOMENT OF MEDITATION

We don't own our memories. They own us.
—Federico Fellini

When the Padre
tells us to bow our heads
and close our eyes
and think of someone we'd like to invite
to join us right here and now
for supper,

I swear it's
Ida Lupino who pops into my head, Ida
Lupino, for God's sweet sake,
Ida Lupino with her seductive overbite
kissing the face of a Hollywood hero
whose name I can't remember,

so of course I chuckle, then laugh,
then guffaw—until soon enough the Padre
calls off our moment of meditation
by calling me an incorrigible numbnut—and
of course he's correct, I admit it,
Ida Lupino for God's sweet sake,

yet as a boy kept off-balance
by the mysteries of girls and of war
I must somehow have loved her,
I in the dark at the movie
with a sack of popcorn
and a junior-high hardon—

so the moment of meditation
goes belly-up in the channel where
probably—the Padre later will say so
himself—it belongs, and we fill our plates
and find logs to sit on in a circle
that for all its admitted gaps

is not yet broken.

LOUP

in memory of John Charles Erickson

One week ago this small Nebraska river
could hardly contain itself,
lifting the full length of its serpent's body
to meet the rain. Two days ago
I watched my friend
watch his child of ten days
descend into a sea of stupifying darkness,
pebble dropped from an unrequited hand.

*

Now I rise carefully in the jonboat
to read the channel,
one week of undiminished sun
having taken its toll. When the prow
strikes sand I sail
like the bird I'll never be
into the wilds of an unpeopled island.

*

Around a campfire
we poke at the darkening coals of memory,
able to recall only six
of the seven dwarfs. Long after midnight
a voice from a nearby tent
shouts Happy! I am lying
on my back, dreaming the color peach,
lifting the sturdiest portion of my body
to meet the woman to raise the child
too dead ever on its own
to rise again.

PRAYER

Calf's bawl from across the river
reaches the campsite

muted but intense, calf
maybe two months old, maybe

Black Baldy, who knows, maybe
Hereford or Charolais, calf bawling

into the darkness
from across the river, lost, maybe,

or coyote-cornered or hungry, water
conducting the sound, muted

but intense, bawl
coming into the campsite

where, between songs,
we listen.

REFLECTIONS

> *I sat under the arched live-oak by the fire with the pup, drinking coffee with a little whisky and honey in it, listening to the Morse dots and dashes of steam whistling out the end pores of a damp log. That gets to be one of the river's symphonic sounds, like owls and the gurgling of snag-thwarted water and the eternal cries of herons and the chug of tractors in unseen bottom fields.*
>
> —John Graves, *Goodbye to a River*

Mid-afternoon, no breeze
among the limbs of the cottonwoods
whose emerald leaves garnish the surface
of the river: O
where does one sense of reality end
and the other begin?

Because both catfish and carp
must be dozing
we lie in the shade of a cedar
almost dozing. The yellow sand plum,
someone says, is better off
jelly. We others grunt our
agreement. And the prickly pear,
someone says, is best left alone.

We leave it therefore alone. No sound then
but that of the river's purling
as it moves through and around
an assortment of beaver-gnawed
branches. It's not the size
of the dog in the fight, someone says.
It's the size of the fight in the dog.

How long I sleep is a matter
of history's opinion, though I can hear
in the far-off distance the popping
of a homesteader's tractor,
its plowshares no doubt
unfurling an arrowhead, a knife
made of stone. Did someone say, The wild
prairie rose ain't found,
it's discovered?

And what I can't see except in reflection
is the cottonwood seed
as it falls from its remarkable height,
its pausing again and again
on its way to the crown of the water.

IDLE HANDS

Because I was taught that
idle hands are the Devil's workshop
I rest the oars sometimes

when I know damn good and well
I should be rowing,
rest made sweeter then

by the threat of snag or sandbar.
It's the sun too that does it, sun
and an absence of breeze

that reduces the body to a slug
with no place to go and
no one to yield to while going.

With a boy yet deep inside me
I drift with the channel, secure now
being myself, untaught

and dutifully slothful.

YEAR OF THE IDYL

On the third morning, floodwater receding,
we drift in a bright serenity
made possible, we say,
by the flood—its rush, its gloom,
its astonishing rise to power.

Now the calm is so distinct
my boatmate can hear birdsong
from more than a county away, he says,
the current so gentle, so steady
we recline,

leaving Our Lady to her own
easy-does-it devices. When the channel
serpentines slowly to starboard
we don't, Our Lady having opted
to move instead

in a subaltern current that takes us
away from the mainstream
into a meadow so dense
with grasses and foliage and flowers
we neglect our reclining

to sit upright to attempt
to believe what we're seeing. What
we're seeing: yellow daisies, prairie
clover, wild indigo more purple than
passion.

My boatmate deliberately, and slowly,
mixes two toddies,
after which we stand
to clink goblets
to toast Our Lady's decision.

How long we drift is just long enough
for *idyl* to imprint itself
deeply: bobwhite, oriole, brown
thrush, jay. These songs, these
colors, this freshness

must surely be a balance
to the singing of Homer's sirens,
balance we no more see or hear
than inhale
until

Time, says my boatmate, is the channel
we drift in, whereupon
he removes first his shirt, next
the watch from his freckled wrist
to drop it into the current.

Time thereafter, until the idyl ends,
hangs suspended. The channel, so narrow
its shores can be touched, slips cleanly
around this bend and that, God drawing
straight, I maintain, with crooked lines.

In due time, when time revives,
we will return to the mainstream,
confluence that place where water
runs into water. Until then
we cleave this meadow with the bow

of Our Lady, small water
before and beneath her
showing the way, bearing
her up, so unassumingly
urging us on.

RETURNING HERE SOMETIME

And the water here
will be cleaner sometime
than at this time
and the fine sand finer

and the shadows cast
by the leaves on the cotton-
wood less elusive then
at the base of a dog-day sun
more sharply defined

and the yellow sand plums
having held their breaths
these many seasons
will explode their ripeness
into the throat of our
impending evening

and what I say now
I will say then

and your answer with
your lips precisely
parted
will be the second half
of all things nurtured

back to living.

NOT DRIFTING

> *My boy, you've got to know the shape of the river perfectly.*
> *It is all there is to steer by on a very dark night.*
> —Mr. Bixby in Mark Twain's *Life on the Mississippi*

It is enough to be here
at night high and dry
on the riverbank
not drifting,

enough not to have to know
the shape of the river,
not to be rowing,
not drifting,

enough to look downstream
not to read the channel
but to believe that
what you think

you see is what in fact you're
seeing yourself alone in
darkness for a jonboat
no longer drifting.

COMING ON

I don't want to say that I can feel it
coming on, here in this
early-morning tent
with each bone
softly aching,
and even if it is
maybe it's only one hill of beans
in a beanfield of millions.

Yet I can feel it coming on,
whether or not I say it. It's
coming on, all right. It's
moving yet too slowly for resignation
or alarm, but it's moving.

I remember Grandfather coming in
from the toolshed,
blowing warm breath on his hands,
working contrary fingers,
saying to himself more than to me, Ah,
winter. It's coming on.

In summer those hands
on the John Deere's flywheel
moved mountains. I stood
at the center of life everlasting
in lespedeza up to my sternum
watching, listening. And

I could see him even before
I saw him, heard him before
I heard the Johnnypopper
popping, glad tidings in a scheme
that long haul knows better
coming on.

HANDS

And it comes to pass that
somehow
the catfish are skinned

and filleted, white flesh
sizzling now
in a skillet of stir-fry.

So many things happen
so quickly,
so free of abrasion, so

beyond and above all
smallnesses
to convince me further:

I am not worthy. Even so,
I help myself
to the stir-fry, I do

my part to keep unworthiness
intact,
aromas of white flesh and

onion and tubers overlooked
by the Skidi
contributing enormously

to the downfall of my puny
resistance.
And it comes to pass that

somehow the skillet is scoured,
sand and river
and invisible hands, and

the greatest of these is hands.

O PIONEER!

The grave was made beneath the shade of some noble oaks. It has been carefully watched to the present by the Pawnee of the Loup, and is often shown to the traveller and the trader as a spot where a just White-man sleeps.
—James Fenimore Cooper, *The Prairie*

The first white man ever to see the Loup
pre-dates Leather Stocking
by approximately
three epochs, according to a historian
who asks to remain anonymous.

Which purported fact makes my discovery
of the great trapper's grave
less significant, epitaph on the headstone
less auspicious: *May*
no wanton hand disturb his remains!

Deerslayer. Pathfinder. Hawk-
eye. Bumppo. And of course
Hector, dog who having in death preceded
his master was, with tenderness
and ingenuity, stuffed and thus preserved,
his form at the trapper's feet
alert to the trapper's final breath.

Fiction first skewed, then the skewing
stretched, leading me
to lift the graven stone to carry it
no short distance back to the campsite,
words of the epitaph fading
with each laborious step,

until arriving I drop its dead unlettered weight
comfortably close to the pit
where tonight another fire
will mark the beginning of the end
of another story in a litany of untold days.

ONLY THE RIVER

It's a day so far without blemish—
calm, mild, sky
blue as the Dutchman's britches,
clear water moving
soundless over an ongoing
scouring of sand.

At such a time who'd stoop
to measure distance? Already
I can taste imaginary salt
rising from an imaginary sea.

*

I beach the jonboat on a sandbar
peopled with driftwood.
I know everyone here and
everyone here knows me.

Break one rule, one law, one promise
and Mama sure enough will find out,
will smack this little boy's ass
all the way into Tuesday.

*

Not far from an old man
posing as a bleached-out log
I build a sand castle fit for a king.
I could live inside those
minutely pebbled walls
happily ever after.

*

When I loft a small stone into the water
it's not really the blue sky that
shatters. O Mama! It's only the river.

SONG

These Nebraska skies,
they hold me like a mother,
and bring a promise
with their morning light.

When the boy opens his eyes
he sees nothing but sky,
the color blue lightened
and intensified
by a high August sun.

He turns his head to see
his father standing
tall beside him, father
in blue overalls
soaked dark with pondwater.

Like a song that is
brother to your stories
will cradle you
in your longest night.

The boy moves his head
to see again the sky.
It is the water
inverted
he'll dream of when
this present dream ends.

So hold me here
when I have fear of dying,
of changing things
in some unknown tomorrow.

The boy is not dead
because his father
in blue overalls

pulled him
from the water,
with two fingers

missing from one hand
pulled him
from the spring-fed

pond. To be alive
is to be free
of the water your

lungs went swimming
in. And the father:
he seems taller now,

though even so
not very tall,
than he has ever been.

Hold me where
Nebraska skies around me
will tell my soul
your story's never done.

Now when the boy lies
on his belly
in the spring house
he drinks not only
water but also
the life of the unborn
fish. He rises
to stand watching
cold water rise
to flow out of its
trough and out
of the spring house
to lose itself
in a clean and
relentless stream.

And so it goes:
our story's never done.

ACKNOWLEDGMENTS

Thanks to the editors of the following books and periodicals in which many of these poems first appeared:

Red Rock Review: "Capsized," "Year of the Purloined Catfish," and "Bird"
Covenants (Spoon River Poetry Press): "Bathing in the Channel"
Drinking the Tin Cup Dry (White Pine Press): "The Others" and "Swamping Our Lady of the Loup," the former reprinted in *Treehouse: New & Selected Poems* (White Pine Press)
Dragging Sand Creek for Minnows (Spoon River Poetry Press): "Loup"
PlainSense (Sandhills Press): "Shoe"
Among the Living (Sandhills Press): "Not Long Before Sunset"
Daily Iowan: "The Deer," reprinted in *Where the Visible Sun Is* (Spoon River Poetry Press)
South Dakota Review: "Love Song at Midnight" and Drifting," reprinted in *Dragging Sand Creek for Minnows* (Spoon River Poetry Press), then in *Treehouse: New & Selected Poetry* (White Pine Press)
Whole Notes : "Returning Here Sometime," reprinted in *Burning the Hymnal* (A Slow Tempo Press)
Shifting Sands: "Eating Lunch on a Sandbar Halfway between Palmer and Fullerton," reprinted in *Burning the Hymnal* (A Slow Tempo Press)
Elkhorn Review: "Mockingbird," reprinted in *Where the Visible Sun Is* (Spoon River Poetry Press)
South Dakota Review: "Wrong"
Meridian: "Bushmill"
Willow Springs: "Instrumental"
Prairie Schooner: "Flannel"
Platte Valley Review: "Coyote" and "Year of the Flood"